The Little
Medicine Carrier

Grace & Truth Books

Sand Springs, Oklahoma

ISBN # 978-1-58339-052-8
First printing (19th century) by
The London Religious Tract Society

Second printing (19th century) by
The American Sunday-School Union of Philadelphia, PA

Published by:
Triangle Press, 1998
Grace and Truth Books, 2002
Grace and Truth Books, 2005
Grace and Truth Books, 2010

Cover art by Caffy Whitney
Cover design by Ben Gundersen

Grace and Truth Books

3406 Summit Boulevard
Sand Springs, Oklahoma   74063
Phone: 918.245.1500

www.graceandtruthbooks.com

Table of Contents

"George Wayland looked at the doctor in surprise."   p. 10.

The Little Medicine Carrier

Chapter One

A Job For George

The lambs of Jesus! Who are they,
But children that believe and pray;
That keep God's laws, and ask his grace,
And seek a heavenly dwelling place?

The lambs of Jesus! They are meek,
The words of peace and truth they speak;
To all God's creatures they are kind,
And like their Lord, of gentle mind.

Dr. Bertram was sitting in his study, busily writing letters, when someone tapped at the door of the room.

The tap was soft and timid, and the doctor was so deeply involved in his writing that he did not hear it. There was another tap, this time a little louder.

"Come in," said Dr. Bertram, looking up from his writing.

The door opened and a very small boy came into the room. The doctor could barely see the boy's head above the other side of the table. Even though he was very small, the boy was stoutly built and his sun burnt face glowed with health. There was a cheerful twinkle in his eye. However, it was easy to see that he felt awed to be in the well-known doctor's presence.

Doctor Bertram put down his pen and cast an amused glance at his little visitor.

"Well, little man, what do you want?"

"I am George Wayland, sir."

"What did you come to see me about?"

"I heard you wanted a boy, sir."

"Oh," said the doctor, and his amused look grew into a laugh as he looked at the size of the young boy. "Do you know what I want a boy for?"

"Yes, to deliver the medicine."

"I'm afraid you are not big enough," said Dr. Bertram kindly.

"Please sir, just give me a chance. I am older than you think. I am going to be eleven."

"Are you really?"

"Yes, sir, really I am. I can read and write and add. Do let me try sir. Please give me a chance!"

There was a confidence in the little fellow that pleased Dr. Bertram.

"Are you a good walker?" he asked.

"I can keep up with any boy my age in Northcliffe, sir. I walked down the river to Norton and back with my uncle last week, and I wasn't tired a bit."

"Now listen to me, George," said the doctor. "You may be right that you are a first rate walker and that you can read and write and add. You may be very strong, even though you are so small for your age. However, you may not be the kind of boy that I am looking for.

George Wayland looked at the doctor in surprise.

"I want a boy who will tell the truth and work hard. One who feels that wasting his time while he should be working is robbing me. I want someone who would ask God to give him grace to be a faithful servant. I am looking for someone who would act the same when I am gone as when I am looking over his shoulder. Would you try to be that kind of boy for me, George?"

"Yes, sir," answered the child with that same confident tone as before.

"You cannot do all of this by yourself, boy," continued Dr. Bertram. "God will give you the strength if you ask Him. Do you go to Sunday school?"

"Yes, sir. I have been going every week for several years."

"I am glad, and I would like it if you continued to do that. You will never have to deliver on Sunday until after church. You can still go to Sunday school and to the house of God."

"Then you are going to give me a chance, sir?" exclaimed George eagerly.

"I didn't say that, did I?" asked the doctor with a smile on his face.

"But I thought...."

"I believe you thought right. I will ask about you in town, and if I am happy with what I hear, I will give you a chance."

"Thank you, sir. When can I find out if you will?"

"Stop by tomorrow night," said the doctor.

"Good night, sir," said the boy; and with his best Sunday school bow, George left for home.

The next evening George Wayland came bounding into the room where his mother was busy ironing. "Mother! Mother! Dr. Bertram is going to try me and I am going to get six dollars a week. I'm so excited!"

Mrs. Wayland was as pleased as her son was, for she had a large family and George was her oldest boy. Even though money was very tight, she had worked hard to keep him in school until now. Very often she could not afford it and she would have been glad if George could have helped earn his keep. However, she knew how important education was to the future of her son. For this reason Mrs. Wayland often denied herself many comforts so George could continue his schooling. One of the neighbors had often said to her, "I wonder how you can go on working and slaving as you do, Mrs. Wayland. That boy George of yours is quite able to earn something. Why my boy Will began to earn money before he was nine years old." But the neighbor did not mention that "her Will" was now a large ignorant boy who could hardly write his own name and who would probably never be anything more than a common laborer.

A child without an education is like a boy trying to find his way through a house without any windows to let in the light. Education is the window of the mind.

George was eagerly looking forward to the following Monday when he would begin his duties for the doctor. His mother was extremely busy trying to get the things he needed to start work. She managed to buy him a sturdy pair of boots with very thick soles to keep his feet dry. Then she made him an excellent raincoat to wear in wet weather. George's father had been a coachman and Mrs. Wayland used one of his old capes to make George's new coat.

As his Sunday school teacher sat down among the boys the next morning, she noticed George's excited expression. "Well, George," she said, "you look like you are bursting with good news. Will you tell us about it?"

"I am not going to school any more on week days, ma'am, because I have a job at Dr. Bertram's. He is going to pay me six dollars every week and I'll be able to help Mother now. I'm so happy, ma'am!"

His little gray eyes twinkled more than ever as he spoke.

That is very good news indeed, George," said his teacher. "I am glad to see that you have the proper attitude about helping your mother. Every child should feel like that. Too often children forget how many years they have been too young to help earn their own keep."

"Isn't George lucky?" said one of the other children. "I have never had a chance like that."

"Perhaps you never looked hard enough for one," said the teacher. "How did you happen to get this opportunity, George?"

"I heard that Dr. Bertram wanted a boy, ma'am. I thought it couldn't hurt to go and ask him about it."

"That's the way to be, George. I hope you will still be able to come to Sunday school?"

"Yes, ma'am, Dr. Bertram told me I should always do that."

"I am very glad, George. You will have many temptations in your new life even though it looks so bright to you right now. I would be happy to give you a little friendly advice now and then. We have known each other for a long time, George."

"It has been more than three years, ma'am."

"You have always been a good and attentive student. God alone can rule our naturally sinful minds. I hope that He will help you follow the lessons that I have tried so hard to teach you."

"What kind of temptations will George have, ma'am?" asked one of the boys.

"I will tell you a few. In the first place, other boys may often tempt him to waste his time. He may forget that his time is no longer his own property when he begins working for someone else."

"Mrs. Oldham, does that mean that George won't ever be able to play?"

"I didn't say that. You know the old saying, 'All work and no play makes Jack a dull boy.' I am sure that Dr. Bertram remembers it too. No reasonable employer would try to make a young boy into an adult by never allowing him time to himself. What I meant to warn George about is thinking that he has the right to do what he likes with his time. I would be surprised if he doesn't have quite a bit of time to play after his work is done. However, I have seen many errand boys waste their employer's time playing instead of doing the job they were told. I thought it was important to warn George against acting like that. Also, in his case, a delay in delivering a package might cause someone to die."

"Oh, ma'am, how could that happen?" cried two or three of the students at once. "A sick person might die, because he needed a particular medicine which should have arrived long before it did. The boy who was in charge of delivering it was playing along the way."

"I never thought of that, Mrs. Oldham," said George.

"Probably not. I only mentioned it to show how important it is for a lad to do his duty faithfully. He can never tell what the consequence for failing to do so might be. I knew of a boy who was sent to the post office with a letter. He was told especially to hurry because it was very important that the letter go out that night. The boy started out, meaning to do what was right. He met some of his friends on the way and they asked him to stop and play a game of marbles with them. He gave in to the temptation instead of resisting it.

The letter, which was a request for a son to come see his dying father, got to the post office too late. The boy's neglect caused the letter to arrive a day late. When the son finally got to the village, his poor father had been dead only a few hours. Another temptation that boys have, when they are in a house where there is plenty to eat, is to steal just a few little things. What does the eighth commandment say about your duty to your neighbor?"

The boys thought for a moment. Then George answered, "To keep my hands from picking and stealing, ma'am."

"Right, George, and 'picking' means taking little things. It is when a boy that is sent for a glass of milk takes a drink when he thinks no one is looking. When a servant takes a piece of fruit out of a pie or a spoonful of jelly from the jar, that is picking.

"Picking and stealing," answered the boys.

"Yes, boys, all of these kinds of acts are dishonest in God's sight. We must be true and just in everything we do, whether it is little or great. When we think about these things, we can see how easy it is to be tempted to break God's commandments. We need to pray, 'Lord, have mercy upon us, and cause our hearts to keep Thy law.' If we are careful about watching our conduct, we will see how often we fail to deal honestly and justly with others. We will find that we do need God's mercy and grace to be able to keep His laws.

There is one other thing that I would like to tell you about boys who begin working. They must practice what they have learned at school, or they will quickly forget all they have learned. If it is possible, they should spend a half an hour to an hour every night practicing their reading and writing. This time will be well spent. I will give you a spelling book, George, so you can practice writing every night even if it is only a few words. When you have filled the book, I will give you another one."

When the class ended, Mrs. Oldham told George to come over to her house the next day if he had time. She would give him the spelling book, a pencil and a small journal. In the journal he could write down special things he wanted to remember.

Dr. Bertram was respected by both the rich and the poor. Mrs. Wayland was very thankful that her boy had found such a good employer for his start in the world.

Monday morning came, and it looked like it was going to rain. In his new boots and thick raincoat, George happily set off for his first day at work. He would come home to sleep every night, so there weren't any sad good-byes. His mother and his little brother and sister all stood at the cottage door, watching him go down the street.

"Doesn't George look like a man now, Mother?" said the next oldest boy Willy.

"A very little man," said Mrs. Wayland, smiling. "In his case I hope it will be like the old saying, 'little but good.'"

When George arrived at Dr. Bertram's house, there was a little pony carriage standing at the door. A pleasant looking old lady was just stepping into it. This was Mrs. Bertram, the doctor's mother. She looked intently at George as he passed her and headed toward the office door. Then she called him to her.

"Is your name Wayland?" she demanded.

"Yes, ma'am."

"Are you the new boy, then?"

"Yes, ma'am."

"Is this your first job?"

"Yes, ma'am."

"Then you can look at today as if it is the starting point in your life, my boy. You are just beginning to journey up the hill. I am nearly at the top. Pray to God to help you run the race well that is set before you. Whom are you to look to as an example?"

"To our blessed Saviour, ma'am," said George. The old lady smiled approvingly at George's answer. She told him that as long as he acted properly, she would always be his friend.

"Do you like animals?" she asked when she saw the little boy's twinkling eyes fixed on the pony.

"Oh, very much, ma'am," and encouraged by the lady's kind manner, George patted the neck of the pretty animal.

"Then, if you are fond of them, I hope you will never treat them badly. I am afraid that some boys think it is brave to hurt and torture poor, dumb creatures, but they are very wrong. A really brave boy is kind and gentle and never intentionally hurts another living thing. He remembers that his Creator in heaven made everything which is alive. Good-bye for now, George. I shall see you again, by-and-by." And Mrs. Bertram set off on her morning ride.

Chapter Two

George's Temptation

George was very comfortable at Dr. Bertram's. The doctor was very kind to him because he saw that George tried to do his very best. The little boy was a favorite with the servants because he was always ready and willing to do anything they asked. The trial month passed quickly and Dr. Bertram hired George.

George had to work very hard sometimes, for he had to walk long distances. When a very ill patient needed fresh medicine, George often made two trips in one day to a very distant part of the area. George was a brave-hearted little fellow who was anxious to earn his own living and be independent. He felt extreme happiness every Saturday night when he took his six dollars home to his mother. This made up for all the long walks in the rain. George had a feeling of satisfaction because he was no longer a burden to his mother.

There were many bright things in George Wayland's path, but he found out that his Sunday school teacher was right. Through his experiences George met many temptations. One of the worst temptations came because of the way some of his former playmates and lazy companions acted.

Naturally, George liked to play as much as any boy his age. In earlier days, he was always ready to join them in a game of marbles or some other fun pastime. His friends either could not or would not understand that now he had something else more important to do and it was his job to get it done. Actually, the problem wasn't that they couldn't understand but that they wouldn't accept the importance of his new duty. Some of the boys knew quite well that tempting George to waste his employer's time was wrong. There are some bad boys who cannot bear to see others better than themselves. They don't try to change their own ways, instead they use every effort in their power to make others be as bad as they are. This was George Wayland's temptation.

There was a hilly road which wound around behind the doctor's house. A patch of stubble about halfway up the hill was the favorite place for the lazy boys of the town to play. They gathered there to play marbles and baseball. Quite often George had to go up this hill, because it was the quickest way to the village of Greychurch. He had to pass the spot where the boys were playing. He had made up his mind to do his job, so he never thought of stopping to play on the way. When his old companions found that they could not persuade him to join them, they began using threats. There were several boys in the group who were far bigger and stronger than George. It was not easy for him to keep away from them.

One day when George was short of time, he tried in vain to pass the spot where they were playing. They snatched his basket and announced that he wouldn't get it back until he had done what they wanted. George struggled hard to retrieve the basket. It was only the sound of an approaching carriage that made them give it up. George escaped with a black eye. Feeling troubled and ashamed, he entered Dr. Bertram's office an hour later after making his delivery.

"Now, George, what have you been doing?" said the doctor in an angry voice. "I specifically told you never to fight with any of the boys in town."

"It wasn't my fault, sir," replied George.

"Whose was it then? I want to know right now." George was a brave little fellow, and he felt that he was old enough to fight his own battles. Besides, he was no tattletale. He assured Dr. Bertram again that it was not his fault. If the Doctor would excuse him from telling any more, it would never happen again.

The boy was so honest and straightforward that his explanation satisfied Dr. Bertram. Although the doctor had a slight suspicion of the truth, he trusted George's word that nothing like that would happen again.

Dr. Bertram's garden happened to reach to the edge of the hilly road where the boys waited for George. There was a door in the garden wall which opened close to that very spot. The gardener was working inside the garden wall when the fight occurred. Attracted by the noise, he peeped through the keyhole just a few seconds before the carriage went by and the boys left George alone. He had seen enough to be convinced that it wasn't George's fault. Since George was a favorite of his, he spoke to Dr. Bertram that very evening. The gardener had seen George's terrible black eye and had heard the doctor speaking to him about it.

"Those town boys are a bad group, sir. I am afraid that they give George a terribly bad time. He is a good little fellow, and I would just like to give them a little of what they deserve. That is, if you don't have any objections."

"What do you want to do?" asked Dr. Bertram. "The next time George goes to Greychurch, I'll hide just outside the garden gate with a horsewhip. Then if they try any foul play, why, I'll be out upon them in a flash."

"You have my permission," said the doctor. "Those boys aren't content to idle away their own time. They try to keep industrious boys from doing their work. That deserves a punishment."

An opportunity for the gardener to put his plan to work occurred the very next day. As usual, George started out with his basket to go to Greychurch. The gardener and servant had checked to make sure that the boys were at their usual place on the back road. Then they armed themselves with whips and took up their post just inside the garden gate. As George approached the spot where the boys were playing, a loud, mocking laugh greeted him. George's face was sadly swollen, and one eye barely opened.

"Come play with us now," they shouted as he came nearer. "We know you have some change in your pocket and we don't have a dime between us. You had enough of saying 'No' yesterday, so come along, unless you want some more fighting."

"I am not going to play," said George quietly. "I have something else to do." And he kept on moving up the hill.

"Take his basket!" cried one of the biggest boys as he grabbed hold of George's collar. The next moment the two strong men came charging among them. They gave three or four of the worst boys a severe whipping that they would not soon forget.

Poor George stood trembling and pleading for them to stop. "They should have enough of that to make them remember," the gardener said. They did remember it in the future. There were many black and scowling looks cast at George. However, they never ventured to interfere with him again if he happened to pass by them.

"I have found that I can trust you," said the doctor to him, "and that you tell me the truth. Keep acting like this and I will always be your friend."

Some time later another temptation came to George. He walked through his little sister's room on his way to bed one night. He stopped to give her a good-night kiss as usual. George noticed that Nelly's cheeks were very hot, and her eyes looked unnaturally bright.

"My head hurts so bad, George," she said, "and I am so thirsty."

Her brother went back downstairs to tell his mother. All that night poor, little Nelly had a burning fever. Dr. Bertram came to see her in the morning and said she had scarlet fever. George went home during the day to bring her some medicine. By then the child was constantly complaining that she was so thirsty that her throat burned. Her mother had brought her some toast and water, but Nelly wanted some oranges. She asked George to get her some.

"If you give me some money, Mother, I will bring some back for her."

"I don't have a penny in the house, George. I paid the last of my money this morning for rent. She must wait until tomorrow."

"I wish I had some money," thought George as he went back to Dr. Bertram's. "Nelly shouldn't have to wait so long for the oranges. If only I had some money."

"Take this medicine to the pastor's house, George," said the doctor as George walked into his room. "Stop in the dining room on your way out. You will see a newspaper on the table. Take it with you and leave it with the medicine."

George did as he was told. There was no one in the dining room. As he went near the table where the newspaper lay, he saw a large dish filled with oranges lying upon the counter. Suddenly a thought came into his mind. "They will never miss one, and I can leave it for Nelly as I come back from the pastor's house."

Who was it that put this thought into George's heart? It was Satan. He is always watching for an opportunity to tempt us to do wrong. Let's remember that it is not a sin to be tempted. Even our blessed Saviour was tempted by the devil in the wilderness. The sin is when we give in to the temptation and listen to Satan's clever persuasions to do wrong. He can never force us to do something wrong. Don't forget that.

He may put the sin in front of us in the most tempting way and use powerful arguments to persuade us that we are doing what's right, but that is where his power ends. He can never force us to give in to temptation. We only do that by our own free choice. If we give in to temptation, it is because we have not asked for God's strengthening grace to help us overcome it. "Greater is He that is in you than he that is in the world," says John.

The Holy Spirit of God is far greater and more powerful than the "prince of this world." God's grace is enough for us to conquer every temptation that the evilness of Satan may devise.

George could not make up his mind as he stood at the table. "It is not for you, it is for your sick sister," was the evil thought that came into his mind. This was the strongest part of the temptation. It didn't sound like a crime when somebody else besides the thief benefited from the act. George's conscience was faithful and alert. It reminded him of a conversation he had a long time ago with his Sunday school teacher about this same subject.

"Don't let any false arguments mislead you, George," she had said. "It can never be right to do wrong." "And I know it's wrong," he thought, "to take what is not my own."

Then the image of his sick, little sister came before his eyes. He knew how comforting an orange would be to her and again he wavered. This time, however, he asked God for help. "Oh Lord, give me grace to do what is right," he silently prayed. He had barely thought the words when the Lord answered his prayer. The whole sin stood out in front of him in all its blackest colors. By God's grace he was able to see all the evil of the temptation that he had about given in to. He no longer hesitated. George didn't trust himself with another look at the oranges. He picked up the newspaper and left the room to finish his errand to the pastor. He felt like someone who has barely escaped a tremendous danger. His heart filled with gratitude for the one who had delivered him.

On his way back, the road passed by his mother's cottage. There was a pony carriage standing at the door. He watched Mrs. Bertram get into it and drive off as he approached. He went into the cottage for a moment to ask about Nelly. What made the color rush into his cheeks as he glanced at the table? On it was a small basket of oranges!

"George, wasn't that kind of Mrs. Bertram," said his mother.

"The doctor told her about poor Nelly's illness, and just now she came over to bring some oranges. That's the very thing the child has been longing for all day."

For several moments George could not speak and tears stood in his eyes.

"What's the matter, George?" asked Mrs. Wayland. "Don't you feel well?"

"Oh, yes. I feel quite well, dear mother. I'm so thankful! I will tell you all about it this evening. I can't stay any longer now."

When he went home that night, Nelly had fallen into a refreshing sleep. The mother and son sat by the fire after supper, and George told her all that had happened to him that afternoon. He explained to her how he was tempted. Then he told her that he was so very grateful that God gave him the strength to overcome it.

"You do not know how I felt, Mother, when I came in and saw the basket of oranges on the table.

It was dreadful to think of how close I came to becoming a thief. Think of how I would have felt then."

"God has been very good to you, my dear boy," replied his mother. "You can never be too grateful to Him and neither can I." She added, "My prayer for you has always been that you will be an honest, faithful boy. We may be very poor, George, but honest poverty is no crime. When we keep our good reputation, we have what the Bible tells us is better than great riches."

"That George is such a grateful little fellow," Mrs. Bertram said to the doctor the next day. "I took his sister a few oranges yesterday afternoon and today he has been doing so much for me. I like to see boys show such good attitudes."

Mrs. Bertram barely knew all that George was feeling in his heart.

Chapter Three

Envy in His Heart

The village of Greychurch lay so close to Northcliffe, where Dr. Bertram lived, that they almost joined. Greychurch consisted of a number of secluded houses, each standing in its own pretty area. There was an ancient church covered with mosses and ivy and surrounded by fine, old elm trees. There was a large pond with luxuriant evergreens planted along its banks. In Greychurch the fuchsias grew to be almost the size of trees and myrtle covered the cottages. The place was a favorite spot for invalids to live during the winter. They rented many of the finest houses for that purpose.

One day shortly after George began working for Dr. Bertram, he saw a traveling carriage. It was going up the steep hill which led into Greychurch. A bus filled with servants and a large quantity of luggage followed it. The carriage belonged to a gentleman who had rented Myrtledene, one of the largest houses in Greychurch, for the winter. George Wayland had gone to take some medicine to Mrs. Mason, the person in charge of Myrtledene. She lived in a small cottage behind the grand house. She was in the housekeeper's room getting everything ready for the family's arrival, when the traveling carriage entered the gates. George had stayed to visit a little with her, because she was one of his mother's oldest friends.

The window of the room faced the courtyard, so he could easily see the new arrivals. A fine-looking gentleman with gray hair stepped out of the carriage. He was followed by a very pale-looking, young lady wrapped in velvet and furs. The lady leaned on the arm of the old gentleman and she seemed to have difficulty walking. After they entered the house, the bus drew up to the door. It extremely amused George to watch the luggage being unloaded. He was pleased the most however, by a large, wicker cage that one of the servants brought from inside of the bus. In it were a pair of doves. A man led a little dog on a leash. A kind-looking, old nurse carried another cage which held the prettiest green bird that George had ever seen. It had a bright red beak and a tuft of golden feathers on the top of its head. George was very fond of all types of animals and birds, and it delighted him to see so many pets.

"Oh, Mrs. Mason," he cried, "who owns all those beautiful creatures?"

Mrs. Mason was talking to a new servant who had just arrived. The servant heard George's question and answered, "They all belong to Miss Beatrice. She has many more at home, believe me."

George sighed. For months he had been saving as much money as he could. He wanted to buy a cage for a young blackbird that a neighbor had promised him. He still had nowhere near enough money. When he saw all these treasures which belonged to just one person, a feeling of envy entered his heart.

"She has all those beautiful things," he thought as he walked back to Northcliffe, "and I don't have anything."

There was more medicine than usual to deliver that day, and George made several long trips. It was very wet and cold, and his envy and self-pity made the bad weather feel twice as unpleasant. By the time George finished his day's work and trudged home, the usual twinkle had left his eye. A gloomy expression had replaced it. His mother noticed the change because even though he was tired sometimes, he usually looked cheerful when he got home at night.

"Are you sick, George?" she asked.

"No, Mother."

He must have been sick in his mind if he wasn't sick in his body. Otherwise he would never have answered in such a sulky tone. He went and sat by the fire. When his little sister eagerly came to play their regular game, he growled at her. "Can't you leave me alone, Nelly?" he said, "Can't you see I don't feel like playing?"

The child drew back with hurt feelings. Mrs. Wayland watched her son with mixed feelings of surprise and sorrow as he sat pouting in the chimney corner.

She waited until all the children were in bed before she spoke to him. She scooted her chair across from him in front of the fire and took out her sewing. Usually this was the time when George told his mother all that had happened to him during the day. This evening, however, he sat moody and silent.

"Here's a penny to put towards the blackbird cage, George," said his mother. "Mrs. Bertram paid me her wash bill today and there was a penny left over that she wouldn't take back. I thought you should have it. How much do you have now?"

"I only have one dollar and two quarters," he said, "but thanks for the penny.

"So how much does that make all together?"

"That makes one dollar and fifty-one cents."

"Then you're more than half way! I'll tell you what. We can save a dime from your paycheck every week when you bring it home. Then you should have your cage before Christmas. Would you like that?"

Mrs. Wayland touched George's head as she spoke. "He's tired," she thought. "He's probably been working very hard all day."

Her kindness made George come to his senses. He knew very well how important even a dime a week was to his mother. His conscience made him feel guilty for his self-pity. He laid his head on his mother's lap and burst into tears.

She didn't scold him. Instead she asked in a comforting voice, "What's the matter, George? Tell me all about it."

The boy told his mother everything. He told her all about Miss Beatrice and her pets, and how when the envious feeling had begun, he had encouraged it instead of trying to stop it.

Happy children are those who have parents who sympathize with them in all their little joys and sorrows. Happy parents are those who have children who confide in them and look upon them as their closest friend on earth. Who else but a parent really has their child's primary interests at heart? Who else is better able to give advice in difficult situations? All people--whether boys or girls, or young men and women--go to your parents with all of your troubles and fears. Don't keep any secrets from them. They have a right to your trust and they will give you worthwhile advice. Many foolish girls have lived to regret the day when they asked a foolish friend for advice instead of their mothers. Many young men would have been saved from a dangerous path if they had made a friend of their earthly parent whom their heavenly Creator had placed over them.

Mrs. Wayland wasn't a scholar, but it is a mistake to think that only scholars can talk well or give good advice. Her heart was in the right place and she loved her children dearly. She worried about their well-being. Even though she was a very plain-speaking woman, every word she told George went straight to his heart.

"Oh, Mother," he said at last. "It was your kindness that did it all. If you had been angry at me like I deserved, my self-pity would have stayed, but instead your kindness conquered me."

Mrs. Wayland remembered the words of a poem that she had read earlier.

Speak gently; it is better far
To rule by love than fear.

She thanked God for giving her wisdom to deal gently with her little son.

It would be good if all mothers followed Mrs. Wayland's example. Remember the saying, "A soft answer turns away wrath, but harsh words stir up anger." Perhaps the gift of speech is the most abused gift which God ever awarded His creatures. David called his tongue his "glory." He said, "I will sing and give praise, even with my glory," (Psalms 108:1).

How often do our tongues shame us because we use them for the wrong reason?

James says, "The tongue can no man tame; it is an unruly evil, full of deadly poison. Therewith bless we God, even the Father; and therewith curse we men, which are made often the similitude of God. Out of the same mouth proceedeth blessing and cursing. My brethren, these things ought not so to be," (James 3:8-10).

What David and the apostle James say about the tongue is so different! One calls his tongue his "glory", and the other calls it an "unruly evil." It will be either one or the other to us; it depends on how we use it.

Mothers, if you speak gently to your children, they will love and honor you.

Fathers, if you speak gently, your wayward sons will hear and obey even your gentlest advice.

Employers, speak gently to your employees; and sisters and brothers speak gently and kindly to one another. If you are patient with each other's failures, your tongues may be your glory. A quick, unkind word, even though it is regretted as soon as it is said, will cause pain that lasts. Slanderous words that are thoughtlessly spoken cause tremendous harm. We must pray for God's grace, so we will not offend others with our tongues. We must not only pray that the thoughts of our hearts are acceptable. We must also pray that the words which come from our mouths are proper in His sight.

That night George had to go through his mother's room on the way to his own little bedroom. Nelly was lying wide awake and she watched George as he passed her. He went over to the bed, leaned down and kissed his little sister.

"I was mean tonight, Nelly, and I am very sorry. I will play with you tomorrow night."

"Thank you George," she said and happily nestled her little head into the pillow.

George's mother wanted some wood chopped, so he got up very early the next morning. He wanted to do it for her before he left for work. He had worked for more than an hour, when his mother came into the yard and saw the heap of wood. George stood there with his cheeks glowing from the exercise and his eyes twinkling with pleasure. Now she knew that his bad attitude had left his heart.

In the morning George rushed to Myrtledene to deliver a package of medicine.

"Go as fast as you can, George," said the doctor as he handed him the package. "I want this to get there as soon as possible."

It was raining very hard, as hard as it had been the day before. George felt strong and happy inside, and he did not slow down. That morning he had prayed and asked God to make him content and grateful for the many blessings he had. He followed the advice his Sunday school teacher had given him once when she was talking about self-pity.

She said, "If people were half as quick to count their blessings as they are to pout about their troubles, there would be a lot more thankfulness in the world. Take my advice, George whenever you feel like grumbling, start counting all the blessings God has given you. You will find there are many others in the world who are far worse off than you."

As he walked along in the wind and rain, Mrs. Oldham's advice came back to him. He thought, "I was very wrong to pout like I did last night. I am healthy and strong, and that's a big blessing. Why, if I didn't have that, I couldn't help my mother. I would be a burden to her like poor Tom Davis is. He is an invalid and has to lie down all the time. If the neighbors didn't pity him and help pay his bills, he would have to go to the workhouse. Then there's my mother. She's such a wonderful blessing! When I saw Jack Brooks the other day, he was wearing old, worn-out shoes and a tattered jacket. He earns as much money as I do, but his mother doesn't care how ragged he is. I know Mother has needed a warm shawl for a very long time. She always gives up things for herself, so we can be comfortable. Besides that, I also have a good employer. I certainly do. I would match Dr. Bertram against any other man in Northcliffe."

By the time George listed all these blessings, he was far more certain that he had acted improperly the night before. He decided to try to do much better in the future. On he walked. His funny appearance would have amused anyone walking behind him. A very large umbrella completely hid the little boy, except his boots. He kept on walking, and just before he reached Greychurch, a man on horseback came quickly riding up.

"Are you the doctor's delivery boy?" he shouted.

"Yes," replied George.

"Then hurry with the medicine, because Miss Beatrice has become much worse. I'm going for the Doctor now."

When George reached Myrtledene, he went straight to the housekeeper's room, because he had a message for Mrs. Mason from his mother. The house seemed to be in a state of uproar. Servants were running back and forth as if there was something very strange going on in the hallway.

"Here, boy! Give me the medicine. You sure took a long time! I bet you stopped to play on the way."

"No, I didn't," cried George. He turned very red and was about to answer very proudly. He made a successful effort to contain himself, however. In a gentler voice he added, "I came as fast as I could, and I didn't waste a minute."

The nurse left before George finished speaking. When he got to the door of the housekeeper's room, he ran into the little dog he had seen the day before. It was whimpering sadly. George leaned down and patted the poor animal. It cheered up a little and followed him into the room.

"Poor Fido," said Mrs. Mason. "He loves his mistress so much that he can't stand to be without her. The poor lady is so sick today however, that they had to keep the dog out of her room."

"Is she this sick very often?" asked George.

"Very often. I am told that she has hardly been well a week since she was born. She suffers terribly, but she is so kind and patient that it is a pleasure to wait on her."

George didn't answer. He was busy thinking about what had happened the day before.

"I envied Miss Beatrice so much," he thought. "I have been so foolish and wrong."

Chapter Four

Miss Beatrice

There was now hardly a day George didn't go to Mrytledene once or twice. Miss Beatrice was very sick. The long, tiring journey was too much for her. It took a long time for her to recover from its bad effects. Finally she gained enough strength back to be able to take a ride through the courtyard in a reclining carriage. Once or twice George met her in the courtyard while he was delivering her medicine. Fido and George had become good friends by now and the little dog recognized him immediately. Fido dashed from the side of his young lady's carriage and jumped up on George licking his hand. At first George was afraid that it would upset Miss Beatrice because her dog had run to a stranger. Instead she smiled kindly and seemed pleased that George noticed Fido. The second time they met, she asked the driver to stop. She signaled George to come over and talk to her.

"You and my little dog seem to have become quite good friends," she said in a very low, gentle voice. "Are you fond of dogs?"

"Oh, I love them, ma'am," said George, and he bowed politely.

"I thought so, because Fido doesn't pay attention to anyone who won't pet him. How come he knows you so well? Do you see him very much?"

"I see him every day, ma 'am, and sometimes twice a day."

"Do you come here every day? What do you bring?"

"I bring medicine, ma'am. I think it is for you," said George as the color rushed to his face.

"I am afraid that I am a great deal of trouble to you. You must be very tired."

"I am very strong," said the little boy. "It's not hard at all to walk to Greychurch and back. Why, once I even walked all the way to Norton and back with my uncle."

Miss Beatrice didn't know the neighborhood very well. She guessed that it must be a very long way to Norton, because George seemed so proud of his accomplishment.

"What is your name?" she asked.

"George Wayland, ma'am. I'm the medicine deliverer for Dr. Bertram."

When George said this, it was easy to see that he felt very important. He was needed very much in Northcliffe in spite of his small size.

"I envy you, George," said the young lady, "when I hear you talk about being able to walk so far without getting tired. I know it is very wrong to complain, because our heavenly Creator knows what is best for each of us. It must be good for me to be afflicted, since He has sent this trial. However, I have longed to be able to run around like other children do. I have never known what it is like to walk just a little ways without getting tired."

It surprised George when Miss Beatrice revealed that she envied him. He was only a poor boy who had to wait months and months to save up two dollars for a blackbird's cage! She talked about being unable to run like other children. This made George remember the happy, free feeling he got from running and jumping with all his young strength. It made George very sad when he looked at the young lady's pale face as she sat in the carriage.

"That's so sad!" he said, almost in a whisper. Again that sweet smile came to Miss Beatrice's face.

"Don't be so sad, George. It could have been far worse. I can't stop to talk any longer today," she added. "I will see you again soon however, and then I will show you my pet birds."

"I've already seen them once, ma'am," cried George. "They are beautiful! The two gentle doves and that wonderful, green bird with the red beak."

"You seem to have picked all of my favorites," she said. "Good-bye now." As she drove off, George took off his cap and made a low bow.

"That is one of nature's little gentlemen," said Miss Beatrice to herself.

"Nonsense!" some of my readers may exclaim. "George Wayland isn't a gentleman? That's nonsense!"

Stop a moment. What is the real meaning of the word "gentleman?" A gentleman means one who is gentle, a gentle man. It means a kind, loving, sweet tempered, polite, peaceful member of society. Whether rich or poor, it is within every man's power to earn this title. It's possible to be rich, wear fine clothes and live in a fine house, yet not be a true gentleman. On the other hand, even poor people can be true, Christian gentlemen. The poorest boy is capable of being polite and kind. Both of these qualities show a gentle spirit.

Whenever I travel through a village, the first thing I notice is how its boys and girls behave. It is a good sign when I see children taught to be polite and respectful to adults. A bow, handshake, or other common courtesy costs nothing. The child who, at an early age, makes it a habit to use these little marks of politeness has already gained one of the outward signs of a gentle upbringing. Don't ever forget that the Apostle Paul speaks of gentleness as proof that God's Holy Spirit is dwelling in our hearts.

After the first time George saw her, Beatrice only went outside a few times. The cold weather set in early that year and Dr. Bertram said that she must stay in the house until spring. She kept her promise to George however. She sent for him one day while he was making his usual visit with her medicine.

The little boy looked with wonder at all the beautiful things that surrounded Miss Beatrice. Her father had given her everything that money could buy so her illness would be easier to bear. There were birds, flowers, pictures and books. George had never seen so many beautiful things at one time, and his face showed his surprise.

The young invalid was lying on the sofa because she couldn't sit up without getting very tired. As she lay there, her cheeks were bright red and her eyes sparkled. George thought she could not be very sick, for she looked so healthy and well. He did not know that those bright eyes and rosy cheeks were some of her worst symptoms.

George played with Fido and admired the pretty green bird named Maco. Maco was perched on the young lady's finger and wouldn't let anyone else touch him. Since the doves were much tamer, George took the soft, gentle creatures in his hands. Then Miss Beatrice showed George a large book full of colored pictures of every kind of bird.

The nurse told George that the young lady had talked enough for now and he couldn't stay any longer. Miss Beatrice said he could take the large book downstairs and look at it. George's eyes shined with pleasure as he thought about looking at all the bird pictures in the book. He was just about to pick the book up when a thought struck him.

"You may be needed at Northcliffe. Your time isn't your own. It's the doctor's." He put the book down.

"What's the matter, George?" said Miss Beatrice. "Don't you feel like looking at the pictures?"

"Oh, yes. Indeed I do! I would like that better than anything, but...."

"What?"

"Dr. Bertram might be needing me and there isn't any way of knowing. Besides...."

"Besides what, George?"

"My Sunday school teacher told me that my time isn't my own anymore," said George, casting a longing look at the book.

"They were very right to tell you that, George, and I was very wrong to tempt you to forget it. You had better go now. I will ask the doctor if you can stay some day to see the pictures. I'm sure he will let you when he hears how faithful you have been."

As George walked back to Northcliffe, he was happier than if he had seen all the picture books in the world. He knew that he had done his job. When he entered the office, Dr. Bertram was just wrapping up a package of medicine.

"Here, George. You are just the person I want. Go as quickly as you can to Earlswood. It is extremely important that this gets there as soon as possible."

As he passed the kitchen on his way out, the cook called out to him. "Here's some dinner that I have been keeping hot for you for a long time. Come eat it now, before you leave again."

George was very hungry, but the doctor's words rang in his ears. "It is extremely important...."

"Thank you very much, Sarah, but I can't stay now. I'll have a piece of this bread though, if I may...." Taking a piece while he spoke, he hurried on his way.

Earlswood was about a mile on the other side of Northcliffe. He had not even made it half way when it began to rain very heavily. He had not brought an umbrella because the weather had looked fine when he left. By the time he reached Earlswood, he was soaked. He rang the doorbell and a servant answered it. A door in the hallway opened also and a gentleman came out.

"Is that the medicine?"

"Yes, sir," replied the servant.

The gentleman walked towards George. "Tell Dr. Bertram that I am thankful that he sent it so soon." Then seeing that George was dripping from the rain he added, "Why did you come out on such a night without an umbrella?"

"Please, sir. It wasn't raining when I left, and I walked very fast because Dr. Bertram said you wanted the medicine right away."

"You are a good boy. Here's a dime for you. Now hurry back quickly and change your clothes."

The gentlemen took the medicine and rushed up the stairs. If he hadn't been in such a hurry, he would have seen the look on George's face. It was a look of pure delight after he gave him the dime. Now he had enough money to buy the blackbird's cage the very next day.

He didn't care about the rain that beat down in his face all the way home. His mother always gave him some dry clothes to keep at Dr. Bertram's in case of accidents. He changed out of his wet things and sat by the kitchen fire to eat his dinner. George looked like he was one of the happiest boys in Northcliffe.

"So, George, you like to look at pictures?" Dr. Bertram said to him a few days later.

"Yes, sir," replied George, but he didn't know what the doctor meant.

"You're even fonder of doing your job, however.

The little boy's face filled with color, because he understood what the doctor was referring to.

"I don't have anything in particular for you to do this afternoon," continued the doctor. "If you would like to go over to Myrtledene, you can stay and have tea with Mrs. Mason. You don't need to come back anymore tonight. I am glad to be able to give my faithful worker a holiday."

Although George forgot to say thank you, his twinkling, gray eyes showed his appreciation.

That was one of George Wayland's happiest afternoons. First he went home, put on his finest clothes and asked his mother to get Nelly ready so she could go along. Mrs. Mason was always glad to see his sister, and George thought it would be a special treat for the little girl. Ever since that night when he had been in a bad mood, he had tried to be kinder.

Since George was ready before his sister, he had time to play with his blackbird. It hung in a wicker cage above the cottage door, and it had already learned to whistle beautifully. It was getting very tame, and it would take food out of George's hand. That alone should show you how kind and gentle George was to the bird. One path to Greychurch led across some fields and through the woods. It was longer than the road, but since there was plenty of time they went that way. George liked the woods and fields most because even though it was winter time, there was always something to find. He could find a pretty patch of dark green ivy or the bright orange seeds of the wild iris.

Nelly also liked the woods. George made a wreath of ivy for her hat. Then they played a game of hide-and-seek among the rocks in the woods. It was Nelly's turn to hide. George just began searching for her when he heard her whisper loudly from behind a mossy stone, "Be quiet, George. Don't make a sound. Come here. Come here!"

"What is it, Nelly?" her brother answered in a quiet voice as he reached the spot where his sister was hiding.

"Look, George, over there in that yellow bush. There it is, just by that bunch of blossoms! It's a beautiful, green bird with a red beak. I've never seen one like it before."

"It's Maco," George whispered under his breath. Then he turned to Nelly and told her to sit quietly where she was. The next moment he was gently creeping through the bushes with his cap in his hand. Nelly did not know who "Maco" was, but she was an obedient child. She knew that her brother must have a good reason for telling her to be quiet. She did as she was told and sat watching him.

He slowly crept toward the spot where the bird was perched. George got within a few yards of the yellow bush when the rustling noise alarmed Maco. He flew and landed on another yellow bush, a short distance away. Several times George almost caught Maco, but he always flew away at the last moment.

Sadly, George began to wonder if he would ever be able to catch the bird. Then he remembered that in his coat pocket he had some bird seed. He had been feeding his bird before he left home. He also remembered seeing Maco come to take seeds out of Miss Beatrice's hand.

"Well, it won't hurt to try," thought George. He spread some of the seed on his hand and went as close to the bird as he could. Then in his best imitation of Miss Beatrice's voice, he called, "Maco! Maco!"

The bird bent his head to one side when he heard the familiar sound. George tried it again. Within a few minutes he happily watched Maco sit on his wrist and peck away at the seeds in his hand. Then George gently took hold of it with his other hand. He scolded, "Naughty Maco. You won't escape again. I'm going to take you back to Miss Beatrice."

Nelly was delighted when she saw her brother coming back with the bird. Now they had something more important to do than play hide-and-seek. They quickly started for Myrtledene. George took care not to let the bird fly away as they walked.

Mrs. Mason was in the cottage behind the house when the children arrived. "Oh, George!" she cried as she came running out to meet them. "Such a terrible thing happened today. You know Miss Beatrice's pet bird, Maco? Well, a careless servant left the window open and it flew away. What?

Why, you mean you've found it?" cried the lady. She glanced down from George's happy face to Maco's red beak which was peaking out from under a handkerchief. George had put it over the bird to be safe. "You are a very lucky young man. That's for sure. They've offered a ten dollar reward for it."

"I'm so glad," said George, "but it's not only because of the money. I'm glad that I found the bird for Miss Beatrice because I know how much she loves it."

Mrs. Mason took the children into the house and sent someone to tell Miss Beatrice that George had found her bird. The happy young lady asked for George and his sister to come up and see her. Then she thanked them very much for bringing her pet back to her.

"Nelly saw it first," said George.

"Yes, but you caught it," added his sister.

"Then you will have to split the ten dollars between you," said Miss Beatrice. The children's eyes shined with delight as she put the money in George's hand. She asked George many questions like where they found it and why they had gone through the woods. George told her about the afternoon holiday that the doctor had given him, and he thanked her for speaking to the doctor about it.

"Wasn't George lucky to be coming that way just then?" asked Nelly.

"Nelly, it wasn't luck! How did it happen that George was coming that way?" said the young lady. "Let's go back a little bit and see. George did his job the other day instead of staying to look at pictures when I thoughtlessly asked him to. If he had stayed, then he certainly wouldn't have got a half a day off. He wouldn't have been in the woods this afternoon, and you wouldn't have seen Maco. I probably would not have gotten my pet back. It wouldn't have survived one of these cold nights. Then you and George wouldn't have won the ten dollars. In fact, none of the things you call lucky would have happened. It all happened because of one thing and that is: George did his job. I hope this will encourage him to continue to do the same in the future."

With that, Miss Beatrice gave George the book of birds to take downstairs with him. He and his sister had a wonderful time looking through it.

After having tea, they went upstairs again for a little while. Miss Beatrice wanted to speak with them. They sang some hymns to her, and she gave George a beautiful Bible and Nelly a hymn book. They said good-bye and thanked her repeatedly for her kindness. That ended George's happy half-holiday at Myrtledene.

Chapter Five

The Gift

"What should we do with our money, George?" said little Nelly as they walked home together from Myrtledene.

"What do you want to do with it, Nelly?"

"Give some to poor Willy. He doesn't have any money, you know."

Their brother Willy was staying with their aunt who lived quite a distance from Northcliffe. She didn't have any children of her own, so she often took in one of the little Wayland's for a month or two. This was an enormous help to their mother.

"I think I know a better way to use our money than that, Nelly."

"What, George? You always have the most wonderful ideas."

"Perhaps you won't agree with me, Nelly, but you can do whatever you want with your half of the money. I want to use mine to help buy Mother a warm winter shawl. I know she spent all of her savings to buy clothes for me when I started working at Dr. Bertram's. She never thinks of herself. Never! Your illness cost her a lot too. When she went to church last Sunday, she was shivering in the cold because her shawl was so thin. So, Nelly, if we... I mean, if I put my five dollars aside and save every penny I get, I can get enough to buy her a new shawl soon. It would be so neat to take her a large present all wrapped up from the store. Then we could say, 'Here is a Christmas present for you, Mother.' I think that I would rather do that than anything else I can think of."

"You can have my five dollars too, George, and then half the present will be mine, you know. I'm so glad you thought of a shawl."

There was only one week until Christmas, so the next morning George let Mrs. Bertram in on his secret.

"If you don't mind, ma'am, I hope you won't think I am being too pushy. Nelly and I have ten dollars. We got it yesterday for finding Miss Beatrice's bird, and we want to spend it on a warm, new shawl for Mother. We don't want her to know anything about it until it's bought. We were wondering if you wouldn't mind buying it for us, ma'am. We would be very grateful."

Mrs. Bertram took the job with pleasure, and George went with her to help pick out the shawl.

She even put two dollars in herself, because there was a beautiful shawl that cost twelve dollars. Mrs. Bertram bought it and told them that it would last Mrs. Wayland a lifetime.

I doubt if there has ever been a happier boy than George was when he received that large package with the shawl inside. He kept it at Dr. Bertram's because he didn't want his mother to see it until Christmas Eve. Nelly would go to Dr.

Bertram's to look at it, and at least once every day they opened the gift to admire it. Sarah, the cook, got to try it on so George could see how it looked. Every night George dreamed of giving his mother the wrapped gift. Christmas Eve finally arrived. Willy came home early that day so he could spend Christmas with the family. Nelly took him up to the doctor's place to show him the shawl. George wrote a little note to his mother in his finest handwriting. He asked her to accept this shawl as a Christmas gift from her children. He used the word "children" instead of "George and Nelly." He didn't want Willie to feel bad, since he didn't have a gift for Mother.

Mrs. Bertram had given George the ingredients for a Christmas pudding and Mrs. Wayland made it early that afternoon. Nelly and Willy were delighted, because they got to help her pick the seeds out of the raisins. When the pudding was boiling and the kitchen was cleaned up, Nelly asked a question. "Mother, can Willy and I stay up until George gets home tonight?" George was bringing the package home with him after work.

"I'm not sure how to answer that," said Mrs. Wayland. "It will probably be very late when he gets home tonight. You have been playing and running a great deal today. I'm afraid you will get too tired."

"Oh, no, we won't, Mother," cried the children at once. "Please let us stay up. Please say yes!" When their mother gave in, Nelly and Willy danced around the room with joy.

Never before had time passed as slowly as it did that evening. There was more medicine than usual to deliver that day, and George had to make several other errands. It was later than usual when he finished work. He put the wrapped package under his arm and ran toward home.

It was a clear, frosty night, and the moon was shining brightly. For hours, two little pairs of eyes had been watching out of the window for George to come down the street. Their impatience amused Mrs. Wayland. "Why are you so excited for George to come home tonight?" she asked.

"We know! We know, Mother," cried the children, "but it's a big secret!"

Finally their patience was rewarded. They saw George running down the street in the bright moonlight with the gift under his arm.

"Doesn't it look big?" whispered Nelly to her brother.

They opened the door long before George reached it. "You all look so comfortable," he said. He gazed around at the tidy kitchen and saw the pudding bubbling over the bright fire.

George laid the package on the table.

"What is that?" asked his mother.

"Open it and see," George said with a mischievous smile.

"Yes, open it! Open it!" cried Nelly and Willy, jumping around the table in wild excitement.

Their happiness was complete after Mrs. Wayland opened the parcel and read the letter. She put on the shawl and kissed all her thoughtful, dear children. She declared that she had never had such a happy Christmas Eve. That shawl was just what she had wanted for a long time, but she hadn't enough money to buy it. They all sat down by the fire and George told all about finding Maco in the woods. He had begged Mrs. Mason not to say anything about the reward so the present could be a complete surprise.

When Mrs. Wayland knelt down to pray that night, her heart overflowed with gratitude. The Almighty God had blessed her with such loving children. Because George and Nelly had unselfishly spent their money, they found pure happiness. It is indeed "more blessed to give than to receive."

Chapter Six

Maco's New Home

It was a very long, hard winter, worse than it had been in many years. The cold was harsh and the ground was frozen hard even at Greychurch, where there was seldom any snow. George still delivered medicine to Myrtledene every day. Yet, he had not seen Miss Beatrice in her reclining carriage for a long time. She was confined totally to the house now. When George asked about her, he noticed that the servants just shook their heads and looked grave. Once when he asked how the young lady was doing, he saw the old nurse brush tears from her eyes.

Once or twice Miss Beatrice had asked George to come up and see her. He couldn't help noticing the change in her. Her cheeks were very pale except for one bright red spot, and her hands looked very thin. Her voice also sounded much weaker. She seemed very cheerful and happy however, and she always spoke kindly to George. She would ask about Nelly and then give George a book to take to her. George could only stay in the room for a few minutes because she would get tired so soon.

"I wish spring would come," he said to himself. "Then Miss Beatrice can go outside and get her strength back." He didn't know that she would never leave her room again until she was being carried to her grave.

Finally the frost disappeared. A gentle, warm wind replaced the cold coast winds that had blown for so long. The birds began to sing and build their nests, and a few brave primroses stretched out their pale yellow blossoms. George knew that spring was near. He gathered all the blossoms he could find, tied them up in a bouquet and took them to Myrtledene. The old nurse was in the housekeeper's room when he arrived.

"What! Primroses, George? Well, I'm glad to see them, for it's a sign that winter is almost over."

"Will you give them to Miss Beatrice?" said George. "I thought they would please her. Then she will know that the weather will soon be nice enough for her to go out again."

The nurse looked very serious and sad. "Miss Beatrice will never go out again, George."

When he looked at the nurse's face, the expression he saw there made tears come to his eyes.

"Is she going to die?" he said, almost in a whisper. It shocked him that someone could die so young and leave so many beautiful things behind.

"Yes," replied the nurse, "she will never get better."

"Did Dr. Bertram say that, though?"

"Yes, he thinks there isn't any hope left for her."

"Oh, I'm so sorry," said George, and tears began rolling down his cheeks. "She is so loving and kind. Does she know that she can't ever get better?"

"Yes," replied the nurse. "Yesterday she begged Dr. Bertram to tell her the truth."

"Now that she knows, is she very unhappy?"

"Oh no, she is just the opposite. She looks happier than before. Her only sadness seems to be that her father is grieving so much."

"Miss Beatrice must be very good not to mind dying."

"No, George. The dear, young lady knows that she is a sinner. She has learned to trust her Saviour who died so she could live. She knows she can do nothing for herself and that Jesus has done everything for her. As a result of this, she holds on to Him with so much joy and peace."

"Do you think I will ever see her again?"

"You probably will. She asked about you just this morning. Dr. Bertram says that she might live for several more weeks."

As George went on doing his work that day, he had many serious thoughts. "How would I feel if Dr. Bertram told me that I wouldn't live much longer? Would I be so loving and trusting and ready to obey the Saviour? Would I feel ready and cheerful to face death like Miss Beatrice does?"

Sometimes it is good to have these thoughts and to not wait to think about serious matters until sickness has overcome us. A good man named Jeremy Taylor said in one of his books: "Think upon dying, and what you would choose to be doing when called upon to die; that do daily, for you will come to that place to rejoice that you did so, or to wish that you had." There isn't a bigger mistake than to believe that thinking about these subjects will make us miserable.

On the contrary, the more we focus on God's love in sending His Son to die for us, the more we will learn the value of His blood. That Lamb was slain and became, "the propitiation for the sins of the whole world." The more faith we have in that all-sufficient sacrifice, the more we are able by God's grace to cast all of our cares on Him. When we receive faith to believe that "He careth for us," our hearts become nearer to God. We will have, "the peace of God which passeth all understanding." Then the Lord keeps our "hearts and minds" in the day of sickness as well as in the time of health. He will keep them in the hour of death and in the day of judgment.

Two weeks had passed since George had that conversation with the old nurse at Myrtledene. Dr. Bertram called the boy into his study and told him that Miss Beatrice wanted to see him and Nelly that afternoon. "After you have delivered the medicine you will find in my office, I won't need you anymore today. You had better get to Myrtledene as quickly as you can."

"Has Miss Beatrice gotten worse, sir?"

"Yes," replied the doctor. "She won't live much longer."

George and Nelly's feelings were much different from the last time they had visited Myrtledene!

That trip had been full of joy and happiness, but this time they spoke quietly and had little to say. They both knew that the kind and gentle young lady they loved was going to die.

When the two children reached Myrtledene, Mrs. Mason sent word to Miss Beatrice that they had come. In a few minutes a nurse came down to take them to her. She said, "I was afraid that my young lady wouldn't be able to visit with you. She has been very sick all morning, but she is doing a little better now. You can't talk to her very long and you will have to leave when I tell you."

They followed the nurse up the stairs and into a room where Miss Beatrice was lying on a couch near the window. When George saw how much she had changed since the last time he had seen her, he was astonished. She gave the young children a faint smile and signaled them to come nearer to her. George's heart was so full that he couldn't speak. He kept wiping away the tears that rose in his eyes so that the young lady wouldn't see him crying.

"I am glad to be able to see you once more," she said faintly. "George, thank you very much for the primroses. When they lay me to rest in the pretty churchyard, will you and Nelly bring some wild-flowers to put on my grave sometimes? It would please me to know that you would do that for me when I am gone."

This time George tried to speak, but only tears came.

"Please don't grieve for me, George," said Miss Beatrice. "Maybe you think I am sorry to leave this world, but God has helped me to surrender to His will. Now I look forward to going away almost with joy. I have not lived very long…only three more years than you, George. I have suffered a great deal of pain, and I hardly know what it feels like to be well. It will be a blessed change for me to go where 'there will be no more death, neither sorrow, nor crying, neither shall there be any more pain."

She sank back in exhaustion from saying so much. The nurse had to give her some warm tea to revive her before she could speak again.

"Once," she said when she was able to speak again. "Once I used to worry and complain about having to lie still all my life and never being able to do anything in the world. There was a good, kind minister at home who made me think differently. He told me that our aim must always be to do what God calls us to do cheerfully and patiently. Some must endure hard work and others must face danger and death for His sake. Some must lie patiently in bed and suffer weakness and pain. This continues month after month and year after year. This has been my duty, and God has given me grace to bear His will cheerfully. I can't talk much more with you now, and somehow I don't think I will see you again. Be kind and loving to each other and ask God to help you always do your duty wherever He places you. George, I wanted to tell you that I would like you to keep Maco when I am gone. He will miss me very much and I know that you will be kind to him. Nurse will give him to you after my death. Now, goodbye. Believe in the Lord Jesus Christ, love

Him, and serve Him in this life. Then we will all meet again in the world to come."

As she spoke, she held out her thin hands to them. The children took hold of them and knelt down beside the couch. Who can tell what God put into their young hearts during that moment of sorrowing prayer? Then the nurse took each of their hands and led them from the room. They never saw Miss Beatrice again.

A little more than a week later, the funeral procession made its way to the churchyard at Greychurch. Some of the old servants, who had known Miss Beatrice since her birth carried her coffin to the grave. This was how they showed their love and respect for their mistress. Many wealthy and important people of the area stood around the grave during the funeral service. Many shed tears as the preacher read the solemn words. "Blessed are the dead which die in the Lord from henceforth: Yea, saith the Spirit, that they may rest from their labors; and their works do follow them," (Revelation 14:13). A little boy and girl stood not far from the young lady's many friends and relatives. They were holding hands and their eyes were filled with tears. They were George and Nelly Wayland.

Not long after that sad day, George took Maco home with him. Since the young lady had not been able to play with him lately, the poor bird had become quite used to his cage. It wasn't a punishment to Maco to stay in the cage during the day. When George returned home at night, he let Maco

out. Maco soon became the little boy's biggest source of fun until bedtime.

George never forgot Miss Beatrice, and God blessed the words she had spoken to him. He continued to serve the doctor very well and was always his mother's greatest comfort. As he grew up, he became a dedicated Christian. Under the guidance and by the power of the Holy Spirit, he walked in the ways of holiness and usefulness. He believed in righteousness with all his heart.

Miss Beatrice's father left Greychurch soon after the funeral of his only child who he had loved so much. He had a gravestone of pure, white marble placed over her grave, and a border of flowers planted all around it.